MR. NOISY

by Roger Hargreaves

Mr Noisy was a very, very noisy person indeed.

For example.

If Mr Noisy was reading this story to you, he'd be shouting at the top of his voice.

And the top of Mr Noisy's voice is a very loud place indeed.

You can hear it a hundred miles away!

For example.

When most people sneeze you can hear them in the next room.

But . . . ATISHOO.

When Mr Noisy sneezes you can hear him in the next country!

Now, this story starts when Mr Noisy was asleep in bed, in his bedroom, in his house, which is on top of a hill.

He was snoring.

And, as you can well imagine, when Mr Noisy snores, that is a snore worth hearing.

It sounds more like a herd of elephants than a snore!

Then Mr Noisy's alarm clock went off.

Mr Noisy's alarm clock sounds like no other alarm clock in the world.

It sounds more like a fire engine!

Mr Noisy woke up.

And so too did all the people who lived in Wobbletown, which is at the bottom of Mr Noisy's hill.

Later that day, Mr Noisy decided that he had to go shopping.

He went out of his house, shutting the door behind him.

BANG!

The door wobbled. The house wobbled. The whole hill wobbled.

Wobbletown wobbled. Even a bird, flying high above, wobbled!

Then Mr Noisy walked down the hill.

CLUMP! CLUMP! CLUMP!

He walked into the baker's shop.

CRASH went the door as he opened it.

BANG went the door as he shut it.

"I'D LIKE A LOAF OF BREAD," boomed Mr Noisy to Mrs Crumb, the baker's wife.

Mrs Crumb trembled, and sold him a loaf.

Then Mr Noisy walked along the street to the butcher.

CLUMP! CLUMP! CLUMP!

He walked into the butcher's shop.

CRASH went the door as he opened it.

BANG went the door as he shut it.

"I'D LIKE A PIECE OF MEAT," boomed Mr Noisy to Mr Bacon, the butcher.

Mr Bacon trembled, and sold him some meat.

Afterwards, Mrs Crumb met Mr Bacon in the street.

"We really must do something about Mr Noisy being so noisy," she said.

"Absolutely," replied Mr Bacon. "But what?"

"I know," said Mrs Crumb, and she whispered into Mr Bacon's ear.

Mr Bacon smiled a small smile, which grew into a broad grin.

"Mrs Crumb," he said, "I think you have the answer!"

The following day Mr Noisy again went shopping down to Wobbletown.

CLUMP! CLUMP! CLUMP!

He went into Mrs Crumb's shop.

"I'D LIKE A LOAF OF BREAD," he boomed.

"Sorry! What did you say?" asked Mrs Crumb, pretending not to hear.

"I'D LIKE A LOAF OF BREAD!!" Mr Noisy shouted.

"Sorry," said Mrs Crumb, putting her hand to her ear. "Can you speak up please!"

"I'D . . . LIKE . . . A . . . LOAF . . . OF . . . BREAD!!!" roared Mr Noisy.

"Can't hear you," replied Mrs Crumb.

Mr Noisy gave up, and went out.

Mr Noisy went into Mr Bacon's shop.

"I'D LIKE A PIECE OF MEAT," he boomed.

Mr Bacon pretended not to notice.

"I'D LIKE A PIECE OF MEAT!!" Mr Noisy shouted.

"Did you say something?" asked Mr Bacon.

"I . . . SAID . . . I'D . . . LIKE . . . A . . . PIECE . . . OF . . . MEAT!!!" roared Mr Noisy.

"Pardon?" said Mr Bacon.

Mr Noisy gave up.

And went out.

And went home.

And went to bed.

Hungry!

The day after Mr Noisy tried again.

He went into Mrs Crumb's shop.

"I'D LIKE A LOAF OF BREAD," he boomed.

"A what?" asked Mrs Crumb.

Mr Noisy started shouting at the very top of his voice.

"A . . . LOAF . . . OF . . ." and then he stopped. And then he thought.

And then he said, quietly, "I'd like a loaf of bread, please, Mrs Crumb."

Mrs Crumb smiled.

"Certainly," she said.

Then Mr Noisy went into Mr Bacon's shop.

"I'D LIKE A PIECE OF MEAT," he boomed.

"Did you say something?" asked Mr Bacon.

"YES . . . I . . . DID," shouted Mr Noisy at the very, very top of his voice.

"I . . . SAID . . . I'D . . . LIKE . . . A . . ." and then he stopped. And then he thought.

And then he said, quietly, "I'd like a piece of meat, please, Mr Bacon."

Mr Bacon smiled.

"My pleasure," he said.

So, carrying his bread and his meat, Mr Noisy set off home, up the hill.

CLUMP! CLUMP! CLUMP!

Then he stopped. Then he thought. And then, do you know what he did?

He tiptoed!

A tiptoe was something Mr Noisy had never tried before.

It was fun!

Mr Noisy arrived at his front door.

He put out his hand to open the door, and then he stopped. And then he thought. And then, do you know what he did?

He opened the door – very quietly.

He stepped inside.

And then he shut the door – very gently.

Quietly and gently were two things Mr Noisy had never tried before either.

That was fun too!

And do you know something?

From then until now, Mr Noisy isn't anything like as noisy as he used to be.

And do you know something else?

The people of Wobbletown are delighted – especially Mrs Crumb and Mr Bacon.

And do you know something else?

Mr Noisy has learned how to whisper!